Sara jumped in a pile of golden leaves,
while squirrels gathered acorns nearby.
"Would you like to go to the farm today?"
her mom called out of the window.

It was almost Sukkot, her favorite holiday. Sara liked everything about Sukkot. She liked helping her dad build the sukkah.

She liked baking pumpkin pies and eating in the sukkah with her family.

the VANISHING GOURDS
A SUKKOT MYSTERY

Susan Axe-Bronk · illustrated by Marta Monelli

KAR-BEN
PUBLISHING
www.karben.com
800-4KARBEN

To Peter, who built the sukkah, to Gabe and Johanna, who found the gourds, and to my parents, who shared their enthusiasm for a good story – S.A.B.

To Max and his cooking, to my dad and my grandfather, who taught me how to grow gourds – M.M.

KAR-BEN Publishing
A division of Lerner Publishing Group, Inc.
241 First Avenue North
Minneapolis, MN 55401 U.S.A.
800-4KARBEN

Website address: www.karben.com

Library of Congress Cataloging-in-Publication Data

Axe-Bronk, Susan.
    The vanishing gourds : a Sukkot mystery / by Susan Axe-Bronk ; illustrated by Marta Monelli.
        p.   cm.
    Summary: Sara and her brother, Avi, try to discover why the gourds keep vanishing from their family's sukkah.
    ISBN 978–0–7613–7503–6 (lib. bdg. : alk. paper)
    [1. Gourds—Fiction. 2. Squirrels—Fiction. 3. Sukkot—Fiction. 4. Jews—United States—Fiction.] I. Monelli, Marta, ill. II. Title.
PZ7.A96153Van 2012
[E]—dc23   2011029820

Manufactured in the United States of America
1 – PP – 7/15/12

But her favorite job was helping to decorate the
sukkah with colorful gourds they bought each year.

Sara and her mom drove past houses and stores and wide, sunny fields until they reached the farm. Their first stop was the petting zoo.

"Hello, Curly!" Sara greeted the littlest lamb. She watched chickens pecking at grain, and fed the goats some grass. Then they went over to the farm stand.

"Look!" Sara exclaimed, pointing to tables overflowing with gourds. There were so many colors and shapes and sizes. Sara chose seven beautiful gourds: three green, two orange, one red, and one yellow. "This is my favorite," she told her mom, holding up an orange gourd. It was S-shaped just like the first letter of her name.

When they arrived home, Sara's brother Avi helped her hang the gourds from the sukkah roof.

Later that afternoon, when they went out to set the table in the sukkah, Sara counted the gourds: two orange, three green, and one yellow. That made six. What happened to the seventh gourd? She looked down. A gourd lay broken on the ground, its seeds scattered. "It must have been the wind," Avi explained.

During dinner, they heard a rustling above them. Suddenly two more gourds fell. Fava the cat raced through the sukkah and started playing with the fallen gourds. Sara counted them. "There are only four left," she whimpered.

After dinner, Avi and Sara brought their sleeping bags into the sukkah. Soon they were fast asleep.

Sara awoke when it was still dark. She nudged Avi and whispered, "I see stars."

"And I see more missing gourds," he said, looking up at the sukkah roof. Only two gourds were left, and Sara's favorite one was gone!

Just then, they heard, "Munch, scrunch, crunch." On the ground sat a squirrel holding Sara's favorite orange gourd in his tiny paws.

"Hey, you!" Sara yelled. "Stop!" But the squirrel ran up a tree.

Sara was angry. "Bad squirrel," she yelled. "You ruined our beautiful sukkah."

Sara was still angry when she fell back to sleep. She dreamed that she chased the squirrel up the tree and demanded, "Give me back my gourd!"

She dreamed that the squirrel came out of his hole with his family and apologized. "We're sorry to eat your gourds, Sara, but we're very hungry. We'll bring you new ones next year."

When the sun rose the next morning, Sara awoke and remembered her dream. She smiled when she thought about the squirrels bringing her gourds, and laughed when she imagined them shopping at the farm stand. Then she remembered that the squirrels had said they were hungry. She ran into the house and brought out a handful of nuts. She placed them carefully in the middle of the picnic table in the sukkah.

The holiday ended, and Dad took down the sukkah.

All through the fall and winter Sara made sure that the squirrels had enough to eat.

A year passed. On the day before Sukkot, Sara raked the leaves on the patch of grass where the sukkah would go.

When you're finished," Mom called from the house, "we'll go to buy gourds."

All of a sudden Sara cried, "Come quick!"

Mom, Dad, and Avi rushed outside. Sara was hopping and jumping and pointing to the ground. There were seven beautiful gourds growing in their yard: three yellow, three green, and one orange gourd, S-shaped like the first letter of Sara's name. The gourds had sprouted from the seeds left by the squirrels the year before.

Sara remembered her dream. The squirrels had brought her gourds for the sukkah, just as they had promised. She ran over to the tree and shouted, "Thank you, squirrels! Thank you for helping me to celebrate Sukkot."